In the Words of Men
Plume Angel
Carry
The Smell of Sundays
Wrapped in the Arms of Ghosts
Lovesung
At St Non's Well
The Presence of Absence
Dandelion
From These Hands
And
Come Back, Mother
Transfusion
Mothering
When
The Gutting of Grief

Introduction

Memories warm you up from the inside but they also tear you apart
—Haruki Murakami

Words run through our entire lives together—in a house, bathed in kindness and memories of love. Words spoken, words written—poetry, conversation, letters, emails, open communication. The books and knowledge of our father—the inspiration and the humanity—all words—so to our dear beautiful Mother we salute you and miss you eternally.

Nicky Wire

In the Words of Men

since you passed,
Mother,
dad and i sometimes
don't know what to say
after the platitudes
stuttered attempts to comfort
'take each day as it comes'
there is a screaming slow silence
that drowns our tongues,
not like the silence of trees in the blue breeze
but an arms open
aching quiet of the wilderness
so,
i've taken to
talking
of my hoped for, yet imaginary
diy projects;
building a garden fence,
skirting board replacement,
B&Q excursions
and the grout,
always the grout.

suddenly,
his voice grows enthused,
transported to hands on reality
a muscled memory
blanket
that,
for a moment,
wraps us in a safe place
and the way
a dove-tail joint
brings two separated pieces together,
or
how sanding with the grain
makes for smoother staining
and of course,
vacuum before
grouting
to give a better, cleaner,
more lasting
fix,
picks us up from the floor
and we walk again
to the next job,
Mam

Plume Angel

recently
i have found
myself
picking up
lost white feathers
like some obsessed
bird collect or i
place
them a l l a r o u nd m e
my wallet
desk,
books
tiny talismans
crashed to
earth
from an icarused flight
piecing together
new wings
for you,

p
to lift you u
and fly away
from this prison of pain
to the safety sky
armoured
by
lightness
and protected
by a
calamus
of
angels

Carry

we each carry
our guises
in hidden pockets
the latent fist
the courageous no
whose words
etched into
fragile identity
those bruises
billowing
in brilliant isolation
stitched
into unspoken
soliloquy
of soul foraged
word hoarded
when
woven
into war
wished away
a million
times
like the
threads
of our
dna
anchoring us
with wings

The Smell of Sundays

especially the afternoons,
my Mother, ironing
listening to the radio,
the archers omnibus or football
steamed up windows
fragments of security stored,
delicately
supremely
safety framed in the freshly folded jumper
waiting for the panic of morose monday mornings
and the drumming dread of
double maths and simultaneous equations
no,
not yet
just the roar of the crowd
on the radio as the ball hits the net,
and the smoothness of cotton sheets
the hiss and swirl of steam,
this contraband of hope
and my Mother's hands
ironing
out
the
creases,   for now

Wrapped in the Arms of Ghosts

like us all craving meaning
who live and have lived
death encircles us
the dying embalm our breathing

comfort or carrion
bandage or burying
the leaving or the carrying
clinging to sepia stained memories
bleeding frames and flickering effigies
hearing voices from forgotten melodies
is yesterday to be our only legacy

cradle me with your smile
deliver us
when it's time
let this
tearblind iris
give me sight
when all i can see
is
the searing daylight

you are tourniquet
when i am wound
you are the stilling voice
if i lose my sound

when the litany of disaffection
plays in my head
you are the chorus of resurrection
reminding me of what
i need to transcend

comfort or carrion
bandage or burying
the leaving or the carrying
wrapped in the arms of our ghosts
wandering in the mists of our innermost
safe in the knowledge of the betrothed
it is with you that i am clothed

Lovesung

catkin, primrose, cherry plum
pussy willow
today i got so tired of
bullets, stabbings, trump, assange and
hashtags
i looked outside
my window
and saw that the sun was shining
and blue was in the air
a shimmering wintered light
held all things new
so i opened my mouth and spoke of you
catkin, primrose, cherry plum
pussy willow
the faded winter colours
carrying tomorrow
in their today
asking nothing
offering everything
freedom sits on the frozen branch
a bud not a gun,
a begun
not an undone,

catkin, primrose,
pussy willow,
cherry plum,
and
somewhere
a bird is singing

At St Non's Well

where edge clings to air
as a baby's hand reaches for love,
a star sun showers winter
with warmth,
where waves batter rocks
send white spray glittering to blue

is this the well we drink from?
is this the silent spring that shudders
the tiny trickles
rivulets of remembrance—
floods—
letting loss
untie itself
and spill to the sucking sea
timetorn tears
wash the want away
mudmanacled fears
unleashed and unbounded
free
now
enough to say
a river of memoria
umbilical to the sea
tourniquet of hope
milk of millennia
flowing expectantly
to where the
blind find the sight
the stammer meets eloquence

the scream,
the silence,
and the imprisoned rise
to transcendence

hold
hold still
still hold
the sea sown seeds of imagination
from the cracks of dislocation
swim now
drink now
hear then
for   when

The Presence of Absence

that   staples   eye   l   ids   shut
stems   shimmer   ing re   l ia n   c e
takes
    a
        tongue
and makes a gag

ghostbreaths   and   shadowcast
ironwrapped lungs
heaving hoarfrost air
the   shallowing of belief

burdened by yesterday

s t i tc   hed   t o   g   e   t   her   b   y
thegapsoftoday,

holes of holiness

punctured throats

sing alone
waiting for tomorrow
to seal the souls
that   once
           stood whole;
whispered words

across the darkdumb night
into the heartheld silence of our lives
lived
living
yet not alive

coated by the patina of the past
just passing through
hold on
let go
sweet lady hold tight
hold
that call to lost love
to come home
come   home
home

Dandelion

from the mouths of corpses
the seeds shall fly
into inside
the ocean is
like weeds eclipsed by flower suns
light will stutter through
wait and watch
the epiphany said
collapse and start again
be a companion to isolation
a friend of regret
a slow breeze blowing through time
a child's breath can mend our sight

the starting clocks of unending daylight
so lay down in seed dawn
away from the deep cut night
the inherent beauty of our scattered souls
searching sacred earth for another place
as
with these holes we become whole

so
fly   fly   fly   away
what we have been is what we are
Mother of millions fathers of forever
fly   fly   fly   away

into the inside
as
what breaks, shall become
for
we are the traces
the traces
left for the next

the next

the

From These Hands

the first touch of love
i remember

the quiet walks to infant school
on rainy mornings in september

helping to write letters on lined paper
the place of a plaster on bloody knees
to make all seem better

the safe sundays of ironing my best faded jeans
the soft listening to my improbable dreams

from these hands
from these hands

passed through arteries and veins of my mother
directing how my hands
may act may approach may reach another

the sad waving at lonely train stations
the happy hugs of repatriation

the placing of flowers to remember the dead in the living room
the handwritten letters
drifting through time for life to improve

the ring upon your finger
a testament to love and sunlight from whittling winter

in these hands   in these hands

the seeds of an eternal spring
the bloom of endless growing
and   the soul
unto which i endlessly cling
with these hands

And

you, my Mother

driving home
just out of hospital
the diagnosis of chronic myeloid leukaemia
fogging our minds
the summer ablaze
all around us

we drive through a broken battled area of town
drunks swagger voices shout
men punch
litter paints the pavement

you look out of the window
warm breeze brushing your cheeks
look at those flower baskets you say
oh those colours just there at the side of the road
i had never really noticed
yes, lilies and pansies, oh they are so beautiful

that
is all you need to know
about   my Mother

Come Back, Mother

i sense a slipping back
away from
overnight
a nottthereness
your beautiful face
filled with worrylines
a going
a wall
a   wan   d   er
in   g
i try to hold you back
stroke your hand
smooth your forehead
iron out the frowns
as once you did to my creases
but   there is a   g a   p
i cannot see
but feel
as if you
are becoming your own Mother
your skin so thin
a fading polaroid
a translucent awning
protecting
a topography of you
sweet Mother
Irene
peace, peace
but you have none today
a silent mantra
offers itself to the world
Mother, come back
come back, Mother

Transfusion

platelets swirl through plastic tubes
a silent rejuvenation
where has this crimson ambrosia come from?
and how will it flow next to your own soul ink
born and bound by wounds
we wash the feet of our neighbours
this maroon sunrise
to marooned arteries
flooding fallow cells with breath
again
energising aorta
through pulmonary   arterial   surge
we write our own histories
through
the gifts

of

an   other

Mothering

shining flowers
stoic photographs
peaceful cards
constant animals
glittering dressing table
selfless heels
writing make up
planting letters
gentle love
blue sense
beautiful worry
cooking hands
campaigning sandwiches
bolstering sadness
building eyes
always curlers
holding others
listening gifs
smiling magazines
soothing thoughts
eternalled now

When

when time was
but cannot be,
hold fast   to time is
secure ourselves
to now to steer   adhere
to the ticking   not the ticked
hands   that hold   not held
and weave the world
as is   not will be

bask in the sunlit garden moment
not yearn for the faraway beach
swallow being whole

for tomorrow becomes
yesterday
all too soon
so embrace the present
the way the sun
illuminates the moon

and maybe the hours
shall fall away
and the seconds soothe
not decay

because tomorrow becomes yesterday
all too soon
the sweetest song
the saddest tune
the dearest love
lives in verbs not nouns
and the everlasting kiss
just this just this
the absolute isness
of our living
so hold fast to now
not the if but the how
as when the sun
illuminates the moon,
because
tomorrow
becomes
yesterday
all too   soon

The Gutting of Grief

plunder this heart
drag me to the edge
drain me out
distil every last drop of blood   into drought
excoriate each atom   of this failing flesh

o plunder this heart
for i shall embroider loss   into my arteries
i shall weave this whittling war   across my throat
and wear it like a shawl
i shall strip myself   down to the bared bones
humility   shall guide my   arrogance

for i do not matter
yet i embody all that matters

i shall be humus
which means - of the earth-
and the rocks and crags lakes and streams
stones and shores   shall carry me
that star light
that breaks through my darkness
is also
your light/ crucified/ and risen
i shall breath to the deepest core
of this molten orb
floating
in the cataclysm of space
and solder sorrow onto soul
i suck the spirits of those
who have passed before me
i wander in their detritus
dreaming their details

piecing together
the fragments of vanished moments
life from the lives
love from the loving

i am inside of myself
from the outsideness

plunder this heart if you must
i let this gutting grief
become a river through me
not a dam
it is in suffering
that i trust
it shall surge and fill
for it to leave me
but i cannot predict
that exit
i have to become the entrance
and the release
to rise in its rising
to fall under its weight
as when
the stomach somersaults in sorrow
my fingers shake in adrenalized weakness
and my tears burn holes in my eyelids
that i know
i know
that i have lived
that i have loved
for grief is the cipher
to pinpoint our acute awareness

from the scorching sun of despair
and to say
i have witnessed
a life
i was there
i have walked that precipice
almost been blinded
at the sight
but but but
in that fleeting flash
that flutter of fury
lived and lives
an eternalling light
that shall sit within our darkness
living
beating on
brightening the shadows

i have lived in the grip of grief
which could only have been
birthed from such sad sweetness
in losing we become all that we once
resisted

for we do not matter
yet we embody all that matters

so plunder this heart

for then
        I know
                it will at least have existed.